NO PETS ALLOWED

Illustrated by
Timothy Banks

Morgan Reed
Persun

Library of Congress Cataloging-in-Publication Data

Persun, Morgan Reed.
    No pets allowed / Morgan Reed Persun ; illustrated by Timothy Banks
       p.   cm.
    Summary : Percy is not allowed to have a pet in his apartment
building, but every time he writes a spelling word, a remarkable
animal appears in his room.
    ISBN 1-57924-077-1
    [1. Wishes—Fiction.   2. Animals—Fiction.   3. Pets—Fiction.
4. Stories in rhyme.]   I. Banks, Timothy, ill.   II. Title.
PZ8.3.P4355No   1998
[E]—dc21   98–18971
                                                      CIP

No Pets Allowed   AC

Edited by Debbie L. Parker
Designed by Duane A. Nichols

© 1998 Journey Books
Published by Bob Jones University Press
Greenville, South Carolina 29614

ISBN 1-57924-077-1
15   14   13   12   11   10 9 8 7 6 5 4 3 2 1

Percy lived in New York City
In a building tall and red;
Each time he passed the lobby,
He saw the sign that said:

**No pets in these apartments—
No dogs, no cats, no fish.**

But there was nothing in the rule
That said Percy couldn't wish.

4

Once when he was wishing,
Percy wrote a spelling word—
And suddenly before him stood
A proud, pretentious bird.

peacock

He put the peacock in the dresser
Before it made a fuss.

But his trouble just got bigger

When he wrote . . .

rhinoceros

He locked the rhino in the closet
And not a whit too soon—

For in another minute
He had scribbled out . . .

baboon

He put the baboon in the bathtub
And broke his pen in half:

But when he tried to write again,
He made a twenty-foot

giraffe

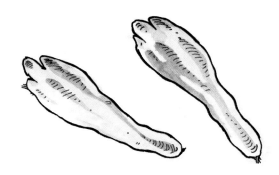

He took the rhino from the closet,
Put the long-neck there instead,
And stashed the grouchy rhino
Underneath his well-made bed.

Percy pondered and he pondered
Over what he ought to do,
And before he thought to stop himself,
He'd written . . .

kangaroo

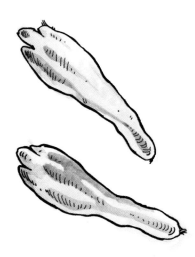

13

He put the kanga in the toy box
To play with model cars;

And before you'd even guess it,
He had written down

jaguars

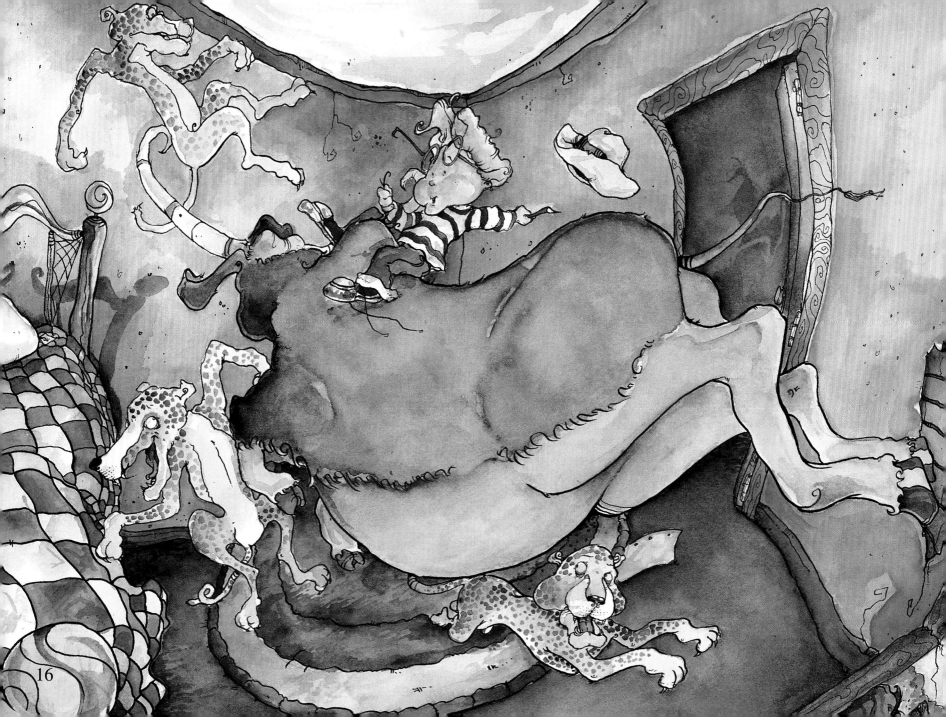

16

There they were, the jaguars,
And he couldn't take them back.
So to keep from being eaten
Percy wrote himself a . . .

yak

The yak held off the jaguars
'Til Percy cleared the shelves;
Then he sat the jaguars up there
Saying, "You behave yourselves."

The yak he tied with shoestrings
To the chair beside the door;
And just a moment later
He wrote down dinosaur

19

He moved the kanga to the bathroom,
Put the baboon in the box,
Took the rhino to the wardrobe,
And he locked the double locks.

But the dinosaur was lonely,
Went wherever Percy went;
So Percy penned a friend for him:
A helpful

elephant

21

Percy yodeled to the dino,
Stroked the elephant on the head,
And he got them both to napping
On the rug beside the bed.

For a moment there was quiet;
For a moment there was peace;
Then Percy made a sad mistake—
He tried to spell out

geese

25

With six birds in his left hand,
Percy tried with all his might
To write another something
That he hoped would set things right.

But instead of writing firmly:
You all must leave the house
Percy found that he had written,
You all must leave the

mouse

What followed was an uproar,
With the elephant in charge;
Now somewhere in the city,
There's a dinosaur at large.

The rhino and the jaguars,
The kanga and the yak,
Every beast and fowl stampeded,
And they're never coming back.

29

Percy watched them from his window,
That squawking, blaring crowd—
And he now no longer wishes
There were animals allowed.